The Ever

Changing

Dream

Foreword

Stand and behold things are not as they seem

As you enter the world of the ever-changing dream

Tales ever captured, summoned to be told

Lessons to be learned, mysteries unfold

A meeting of the mind, sail upon the shore

A journey to be ventured, ever filled with awe

Puzzles of amazement, one shall so discern

Rise above the fear and so you may return

Chapter One

Jesse Jobson peered out his bedroom window, gazing into the distance, yet entranced in a field of dreams. The night had worn on, but the still of the night had not kept him from seeking, nor staring, nor searching.......for that solution.

'Tap, tap, tap', there were three familiar knocks at his door.

"Jesse, I trust that one is sleeping, for there is school in the morning." A gentle reminder of the day ahead from his endearing and ever-enthusiastic mother Suzie. On the contrary, his father Jimmy was of the more laidback kind, yet stern with respect to his dealings of daily life.

Somewhat timid in nature, Jesse's days in the midst of parental guidance, were often spent either trying to please or trying to prove accomplishment. Yet in the face of daily trials and personal challenges, his journey was soon to be accompanied with valued assistance by an unfamiliar fellow.

With a new day begun, came the rising of the sun, yet Jesse lay heavy asleep. 'Tap, tap, tap', there were the knocks at the door.

"Jesse, I trust that you've showered and brushed your teeth, your breakfast awaits you at the table."

"Hmmm, hmmm," mumbled Jesse, still half in a daze.

"I'll be down in a minute."

The clock hand had turned another quarter, but there was still no sign of Jesse. He had continued to lie under his duvet, in waiting for but a dreaded time. For Jesse the school day ahead meant on-going trials with unfamiliar rivals, who sought to spoil the experiences of anyone they regarded as inferior. The majority of his classmates were of the friendly kind, yet there were also the few whose aim it was to disturb the peace of the day. Jesse was therefore in no hurry to vacate his haven and begin his journey to the school gates on time.

On this occasion there was to be no more friendly taps at the door, only amplified rage in order to hurry Jesse along. "Jesse Jobson, for the last time, GET A MOVE ON OR YOU'RE GOING TO BE LATE!!!" Jesse jumped to attention at once, making a desperate dash to the bathroom to carry out a very rushed routine. The moments that followed saw Jesse scurrying down the stairway like a one-armed bandit, with one sleeve hanging loose, toast at the teeth and his tie stuffed into his trouser pocket. In all manner of disarray he followed his mother to the car, who was anxious to get going, as tardiness was not her forte.

Suzie's royal red car was in need of repair, although several scratches later, she still deemed it to be ready and reliant. She was always fond of her ready Rebecca, but to Jesse he felt continued bouts of shame whenever he was seen by his peers in his mother's beloved rusty car. 'Cluck, cluck, cluck' came the sound of the exhaust as they pulled up outside the pearly purple gates of Rodrum Academy. Jesse quickly ducked his head as he caught sight of Toby who was the ringleader of the Uptown Boys. Luckily for Jesse, he sat unnoticed by his dreaded rival.

"Okay Jesse, quick kiss on the cheek now, time for school. Aah, don't forget later, you're walking back home, part of your exercise routine okay."

With Jesse now in the building and his classmates in full glare, it was now time for him to face the music. Fortunately, it was Tuesday and his first lesson of the day was music , with his favourite teacher Mr Dunsall.

"Come on in everyone, take your seats, we'll be starting s-h-o-r-t-l-y." Mr Dunsall who was always besotted with singing and with any musical concepts, always spoke in an illustrative manner. He would often emphasize the end of his sentences with a high pitch or burst out in song, to the delight of many of his students.

"Today, we are going to be watching a video on composition and taking notes thereafter, so I'll need two helpers to assist with the setting up of equipment."

The first few minutes comprised a state of calm, with attentive students tuned in to the screening. The initial calm was however to be short-lived and then came the erupting storm. Chuckles of laughter seemingly came from the left area, but then appeared to be coming from the other side. 'Drip, drip, drip'. Drops of an unknown liquid could be seen funnelling across the floor beneath one of the chairs. Mr Dunsall peered closer to the sight. "What is the meaning of THIS!" Exclaimed Mr

Dunsall with a notable high pitch at the end. He had come to realise that

one of the students had secretly brought in a drink to the lesson, secretly

sipping but unable to contain their laughter.

Although usually a pleasant teacher, Mr Dunsall had a specific way of

imposing detentions on students whose behaviour was out of line. Like

a regimental army officer, he shouted "ATTENTION". At this point that

specific word meant all pupils had to abruptly stand to their feet. It was

now Mr Dunsall's turn to proceed to point exactly to the pupil who would

be designated the detention. He then pointed to Maggie, who had

brought the drink to the lesson, exclaiming "DETENTION", whilst

wiggling his second finger in her direction at the same time. She knew

she was his unwholesome candidate this time for a thirty minute

detention of writing repeated lines. 'I will conduct myself in an orderly

manner, I will conduct myself in an orderly manner.......'

To top it off, whilst the pupils were all standing, another pupil then began

to display a brief dance on periodic occasions. At one moment swaying to the side, standing still, then clicking his fingers and following on with the moonwalk. "What is the meaning of THIS!" Beckoned Mr Dunsall.

"Er sir, I forgot to give you my note from my parents." Insisted Royson, the dancing student. He then presented a bewildered looking Mr Dunsall with a shiny note, glaring at every crease, yet crumpled with every crunch.

"Er sir, it tells you, I've recently been told by my doctor that I suffer with 'danceritus'."

Mr Dunsall appeared now to have become enflamed with fury.

"Are you being real with me? Are you having a laugh?"

"Er no sir, I'm having a dance!"

"Well you won't mind if I take this note and run it by the headmaster later now, will you?"

After such a disturbance, it then took another several minutes before any calm could be restored and the lesson plan back on track.

"I must say students, it is such a SHAME," said Mr Dunsall shaking his hands in the air with all emphasis.

"It is such a SHAME to have instances where just a few spoil the experience for the rest."

Jesse's muddled morning consisted of music, followed by English Literature, break and then PE. At least now he could look forward to his lunch hour and replenish his restless mind.

Aligned in the dinner queue, he now waited to be served after rustling through several trays before he could find a squeakily clean one.

"Well what can I get you?" said Mrs Sunders ready to serve the eager pupils.

"Triple chips, thanks!"

"Triple chips," exclaimed Mrs Sunders. "No not today, we've started a new healthy eating scheme. I can give you triple carrots if you like." Jesse shuddered his shoulders in response and then proceeded on to his next available choices.

The second half of the lunch hour, usually saw the majority of pupils scurry off into their peer groups or well known cliques. Jesse would keep the company of his best friend and loyal pal Daz. For Daz however, a great deal of his school experience included being mocked for not wearing shirts that were immaculately laundered white. They had become befriended soul mates, solely because they were both regarded as being different and somewhat inferior by other less challenged pupils. They had both seen each other through tough times and had rarely parted company throughout their school years.

Both Jesse and Daz had come from modest backgrounds and on many occasions had to 'make-do' with what their respectable families could provide. In retrospect although they had been the butt of other pupil's jokes, they continued to support each other morally and emotionally.

At the other end of the school fields, amongst the crowds was Elizabeth, who stood talking among friends. She both dazzled and caught the eye of Jesse on a number of fond occasions, though not to her knowledge.

She exuded a flamboyant combination of both flair and confidence, which rather appealed to the dozens. Elizabeth was in the league of the more popular pupils since her school life began. Her prestigious father, a highly driven entrepreneur, would always be seen on his arrival to collect Elizabeth in the latest sports car. With such a life of little need, or want, their existing states seemed worlds apart.

As the lunch hour drew to a close, other pupils proceeded towards their respective classes, although not always in an orderly fashion. Jesse and Daz soon found themselves both sandwiched and squeezed between the mass of Uptown Boys.

"Oi you, can you get out of my way?" Barked Toby, in an effort to intimidate Jesse.

"I, I, can't, I'm stuck." Insisted Jesse.

"Well if you were any shorter, I bet I could squish you like a toad." Implied Toby.

"Leave him alone Toby, haven't you bothered him enough this week," said Sid of the Uptown Boys in an effort to defend Jesse.

"Give him a break."

"Give him a break, next thing you know you'll be asking me to give him a 'wafered' chocolate bar," said Toby.

As the mass of pupils still remained muddled, it then took a further gruelling two minutes before an approaching teacher came to separate the crowd.

"Oi Jesse..........until the next time!" Said Toby

After being rendered in a somewhat fearful state, Jesse did his best to keep his head down and 'lay-low'. To continue his aim of avoidance at least meant that he would be out of sight from the Uptown Boys - most of the time.

At this stage of his educational as well as personal journey Jesse existed, but was not yet truly living. The majority of days were spent wishing it away, yet the majority of nights were spent wishing nightmares away. Either way he hadn't yet found the practical solutions to the challenges he faced or how to overcome the obstacles thrown in his direction.

The journey home was fast approaching in which Jesse's shallow breaths were accompanied with a heavy feeling in the pit of his stomach. He was now faced with indecision as to which way he should walk home, as well as which roads to steer clear of. If the Uptown Boys were heading down the high road, he would surely then take the low road.

By twenty past three the sky was clear with radiant peace, yet no inner peace resided within Jesse. In the corner of his eye he noticed the Uptown Boys heading up Turnwell Lane. After a cheerful goodbye from his best friend Daz, he stood still for a further few minutes and then proceeded down Fearson Road.

As Jesse arrived at the flowery front door he breathed a sigh of relief, to have reached the residence of territorial safety. Along with a warm greeting his mother had already laid out healthy snacks at the ready, including sliced fruit and oatmeal bites.

"How was your day honey?" Said Suzie, with a hearty hot drink held steadily in one hand.

"Honey", answered Jesse in an unremarkable tone.

"Well okay, how was your day sugar?" Said Suzie!

"A load of salt, I guess!" Jesse declared.

"Oh poor lad, still not getting on with your teachers?"

"Yeah, I guess not." The current response from Jesse as to the status quo was actually far from the truth. In actual fact he had got on splendidly with his teachers at school, however fitting in with a number of his peers was the issue at heart.

A good while later he scaled the stairway to his haven within the haven, to his bedroom of personal rest from the outer world. He informed his mother that he would now be spending time on his homework as well as a promise of valuable reading time.

In all fairness he did dedicate a good portion of the late afternoon to his homework assignments. As for the remainder of that time, he spent that rallying back and forth in his mind as to the ways he could overcome the indifferences he had at school. There were on-going contemplations as to how he would get through the rest of the week with having to breath the same air as the Uptown Boys, let alone the rest of his academic schooling.

The contemplation count could now be counted to two hours to be precise. After strolling down the stairs to the dinner table, he proceeded to sit down amongst his parents.

"Lamb chops or stew, take your pick my son," said Suzie in a pleasant manner.

"Er, whichever I don't mind."

"Oh dear, are you still a 'tad' bit down in the dumps?"

"Oh, don't worry, I'll be fine, erm, I guess I'll have some of those tasty lamb chops with my tea," insisted Jesse.

His strong silent father did actually contribute a sentence or two throughout the meal, yet even he was too busy contemplating the business day ahead. Although communication and father-son bonding was not yet at its highest level, they deep down have a fair bit in common. In spite of this Jesse always did his level best to get on his father's good side. It had been nearly three years since they last went on a fishing trip together, or any trip for that matter. He longed for the substance of quality time with his father of whom he looked up to in many ways.

The family filled their evening with mugs of cocoa and quiet conversation over the latest soap dramas. "Last one upstairs is a smelly fish!" Insisted Suzie with her dry yet quirky sense of humour! She had been using that line in order to persuade Jesse to retire for bed for several years, without any intention of changing it. In many ways she still regarded Jesse as her beloved baby, of which her fondness continued to blossom as he headed further towards maturity.

Even at this stage in his life she still peered round the door of the bathroom so as to check that Jesse was brushing his teeth correctly. The brightly coloured ducks by the bath was her idea and in her mind she still retained the notion that Jesse still desired ducks.

Chapter Two

On such a tranquil night with gazing stars, Jesse's head was still in a daze, full of thoughts and saturated with puzzles. Would he ever fit in? Would he always feel the need to distance himself? Either way he didn't quite feel at liberty to really be himself in the midst of others. He felt he could only reveal his true character only to himself and by himself in his personal haven. Little did he know he was about to embark on an adventure that would enable him to explore the concepts of possibilities and to harness bold imagination.

'Rat, tat, tat, tat.'

"Oi, who's that?" Said Jesse feeling instantaneously alarmed.

'Tick, tock, tick'.

"Oi, who's this?" Called an uncertain Jesse!

A short period of silence, followed by distressed creeks of his bedroom door, soon saw a glistening green light appear beneath the gap. This very light seemed to have a mind of its own. It was slowly travelling from beneath the door, inching closer and closer towards him as he sat hunched at the centre of his bed. At once this mysterious light with fluorescent yellow dots began to take form.

Exactly what was this strange light becoming? What began as two rays of light soon became two lengthy arms, two spindly legs, two prying eyes. A rare looking fellow had now formed, into an unusual state. A glowing light, becoming a man, how could this be? A light that now moved, could dance, could walk, and could talk! To have transitioned to seemingly human form, yet not of this world!

"Er, I'm feeling frightened right now, but exactly who are you? What are you and what are you doing here in my room.?" Jesse questioned.

"Ay ay mi lad, I know I is a mysterious fellow. Yet you can call me Glad, that is glad to see ya," said the mysterious fellow.

"GLAD, GLAD.........WHAT KIND OF NAME IS THAT?" Jesse said hastily.

"Well, I is not from these lands, I came here from another world, a world you have not seen, but surely can, if you……believe mi lad!"

"Believe, believe in what exactly?" Jesse asked intensely.

"To believe beyond your own limitations mi lad. To believe that one can achieve what one desires and that one can overcome." Glad said.

"Do you always talk in mysterious language? What exactly do you even know about my life anyway?"

"Ah mi lad, I am of the acquired knowledge of many a things and can read many a thoughts. I knows that ye has endured many troubles at school, that ye wants to know his father more. I also know that you would like to [coughs], acquire the friendly acquaintance of a very special girl, Elizabeth me thinks."

"Er, you know that I fancy, I mean, that I like Elizabeth and all about my troubles at school?"

Glad laughed ever so delightfully. "Ah yes mi lad and now it is time for ya sprinkin mi lad!"

"Sprinkin, what do you mean?" Jesse enquired.

With two shakes of his hands, Glad reached down into his waistcoat

pocket, to reveal a transparent jar. The jar at first sight appeared empty,

but was exceedingly full. As he unopened the jar, he reached his hand

into it and sprinkled an array of dazzling dust over Jesse.

"Now fear not mi lad, I is taking you on a special journey tonight and I

promise ya'll be back by morning!"

"Taking me where exactly and how?" Jesse said.

"We is going by glow-light to an ever-changing land of dreams, of which

for every visit you take, you will overcome the very problems in yer life.

There is no time like the present!" Glad then chanted a verse.

Stand and behold things are not as they seem

As you enter the world of the ever-changing dream

Tales ever captured, summoned to be told

Lessons to be learned, mysteries unfold

A meeting of the mind, sail upon the shore

A journey to be ventured, ever filled with awe

Puzzles of amazement, one shall so discern

Rise above the fear and so you may return

Glad gleefully embraced the arm of Jesse in which they both seemingly evaporated from view. Both fellow and friend were now twirling forcefully in an outstretched tunnel of light that appeared to have no end. Further ahead they were approached by flying fishes, heading in every direction. Mysterious creatures of every kind dotted in an out of the tunnel of light, with varied beams of light, ever-glowing, ever-changing colours and directions.

"Almost there mi lad, hope ya like creatures, they are valuable to our journey, ah ha and they won't bite." A brilliantly enchanting light appeared before them, in which they spun at the speed of light in a forward motion.

"Aaah, we're spinning, we're spinning!" Cried Jesse, unsure of what lay ahead.

As the bright light faded they both found themselves stood at the pearly purple gates of Rodrum Academy, to Jesse's surprize. "What in the 'blazers' are we doing here? Jesse said in a state of shock.

"Ay mi lad, this is your renewed version of your day at school, time to sort your problems mi thinks, er and don't look down." Jesse then peered down to find he was actually now dressed in his school attire and soon saw the masses of other pupils arriving in all readiness. This indeed was another world, yet the same world with another chance to welcome change.

Glad reached once again into his pocket this time to reveal a very miniature jar of dazzling dust. "Now lad, this jar is for you and within it contains the dust that will do whatever you command it to do……..if only you truly believe."

"Well, what do you want me to do with it?" Jesse asked.

"Well mi lad, only you and I can see this dust, the other people on this yer planet are not aware of it. They cannot see me either, just only you. So throughout school today, the very problem ye face, ya sprinkle the dust and command the solution in your mind. So we are now going to

have a quick practice right here mi lad."

Glad now pointed to a nearby tree just a few yards away. On

approaching the tree Glad advised Jesse to open the jar and sprinkle a

bit of dust over the tree. "Now mi lad, you must now command the tree

to do whatever you desires it to do and to use your mind, now words,

just your mind."

The first thought that came to Jesse's mind was a vision of the tree

dancing. Jesse then gazed forcefully at the tree, whilst conducting inner

instruction. Moments had passed and to no avail, the tree continued to

be still.

"Try again mi lad, if you don't succeed, try again and all that, just really,

really believe it within." No sooner did Jesse try again and the tree then

began to dance at once. The branches began swaying from side to side,

whilst the torso began to swirl with disco flair. The dancing tree was now

a force to be reckoned with, jiggling from left to right.

With his trial run complete Jesse now entered the gates to begin the school day with hope and faith entwined. Both Jesse and Glad walked together, yet surrounding pupils would only be aware of Jesse alone.

Mrs Gosh, who was Jesse's teacher of English Literature, stood at the entrance of the classroom door to usher the pupils in. "Come along, come along, time waits for no student!"

Upon the class being seated, stood an air of silence, for the teacher demanded such protocol when lessons commenced. She would not allow a wandering whisper, nor a flicker of a pen to interrupt the flow of her lessons.

Following the morning register in which pupils were to answer 'good morning Mrs Gosh', was the time scheduled for silent reading, in which no words were to be uttered aloud. Although Jesse was situated quite a distance from Toby, he was still in full clear view.

During such a lesson Toby's usual way of aiming to get Jesse into trouble was to flicker tiny rolls of scrap paper towards him, in order to create a reaction of uttered words. This time however, Jesse had a different idea of his own. Jesse began assuredly by giving Toby the benefit of the doubt and trusting that he would not begin his usual malpractice. As time ticked on, so Toby then began his first attempt at rolling a small scrap of paper to then throw at Jesse. He managed to fulfil his sorry task on two occasions, yet this time Jesse would not respond with words.

"Go on mi lad, you know what to do." Glad uttered, seated restfully at the back of the room. Jesse raised his hand and asked if he could fetch a tissue from the far right of the room. With Mrs Gosh's approval he made his way towards the box of tissues, but this time ensuring he would be within the immediate vicinity of Toby. As he stood in front of the box of tissues he secretly opened the jar of dazzling dust ensuring that it rested firmly in the grip of his hand. On his way back to his seat he walked to the rear of Toby's seat and lo and behold sprinkled the dazzling dust over Toby.

With Jesse returned to his seat he now had ample time to really believe in the power of his desire, along with the dust. He envisioned an ability for Toby to be unable to stop talking for involuntary moments on end. The entertainment then ensued and before you know it, Toby began uttering all manner of words and erratic sentences.

"I, I, I, I is a professor!" Toby uttered, unbeknown as to why he acted this way!

"Toby, you know there is to be no talking in my class during reading time." Mrs Gosh declared.

"Oh Gosh, Mrs Gosh, you are quite very posh, how about we for lunch and munch on some lovely nosh!" Toby said with all bewilderment. The entire class, although shocked soon began to laugh at the humour of all the utterances of Toby on repeat.

"Toby, leave my classroom at once and go straight to the headmaster's office, since you cannot stop talking."

"Okay, Mrs Gosh, yes you are the boss." Toby said in a cheerful yet confused manner.

Glad then leapt up at once with joy and declared, "You did it lad, you did it, bet Toby won't be feeling quite so powerful now!"

In such a vast school, Jesse was not the only pupil to endure trials and tribulations. From time to time, he was all too aware of specific individuals who were ridiculed, humiliated or treated disrespectfully by others. On this day he additionally wanted to harness the power of the dazzling dust to assist other pupils in unwholesome situations.

As Jesse and Glad made their way down the corridor, they became aware of a young girl with pigtails being continually tripped over as she walked amongst a group of disruptive girls. "Look at her, she really thinks she's all that." One of the girls stated to her peers.

"Yeah, as if any boy would be interested in her!" Another girl replied.

They sought to continue in this fashion, whereby Jesse soon came to the realisation of an assisting plan. To everyone's sudden surprise a frog, simply out of nowhere jumped onto one of the girls and began hopping on one of them to the other. A bout of mayhem soon ensued and suddenly the group of girls became terrified of their new 'froggy' friend and went 'beserk'. Neither of them knew which direction to turn and each one made a dash for the hills.

As the young girl with the pigtails caught Jesse's eye, he gave her an encouraging wink, in which she glanced at him, gave him a small smile and went on her way. "Alright mi lad, let's hop on me thinks, it's time for lunch."

Once again in the dinner queue, Jesse was contemplating his choices, but this time consisting of healthier selections. On this occasion he opted for the vegetarian option. "Be sure to put plenty of peas and carrots on my plate please." Jesse exclaimed.

"Good choice sir and what can I get you for desert?" Jesse stood momentarily undecided as to which choice to make; he was radiantly presented with lemon meringue, strawberry mouse, apple turnover and a selection of fruits.

"Hmmm, hmmm, choices, choices!" Jesse said whilst simultaneously tapping his chin.

"Get a move on, the rest of us need to eat you know!" A pupil said hesitantly waiting in the queue.

"Alright, alright, the lemon meringue it is, haven't had that for ages." Jesse voiced.

Jesse merrily made his way to the seat next to Daz, who was already munching away at his appetizing meal. The Uptown Boys were moving closer towards being served, whilst constantly chatting away about their up and coming schemes. Thereafter they were sure to position themselves in close proximity to where Jesse was seated.

Whilst the majority of pupils would converse and enjoy their meals in a calm manner, the Uptown Boys always felt the need to be extravagant. Their voices had to stand out, whether in the dinner hall, in the fields or in the school library. They would often inappropriately include Jesse in their vocalised conversation, rendering Jesse less able to focus on his meals.

It didn't take long for a pre-selected number of peas to make their way from the plates of the Uptown Boys to where Jesse was seated. The majority of days they just couldn't help themselves with the varied stunts they felt they needed to pull.

Today's lunchtime saga consisted of the Uptown Boys mocking Jesse's school attire with the motive of creating indifference. "So what do you think of his school shoes then?" One of the Uptown Boys asked.

"Not my kind of style!"

"Yeah, much too cheap for me. I much prefer shoes of the more expensive kind." Suddenly in the space of a second, a single penny went flying towards Jesse's school blazer, before cascading to the floor.

"Yeah, throw him a penny, might help towards his savings!"

These gruelling episodes were becoming more and more disappointing and unsettling, but Jesse now turned his attention to the very dust that would dazzle his rivals.

"That's the spirit mi lad, we won't settle for that!" He stood up at once and proceeded towards the corner of the hall where the bin was located. During his visit he was able to quickly unearth a bit of dazzling dust from the jar in his pocket. On his return to his seat he was sure to sprinkle the dust across the Uptown Boys, unnervingly unnoticed. As he sat down alongside Daz, he made the choice to relinquish his belief as to the events that would unfold.

Via his thought process, pieces of fruit would come alive. As a group of nearby students made their way to empty their trays, a number of banana skins made their way from the trays. They slowly slid across the floor to the seating area of the Uptown Boys. They stood up to go and empty their trays only to suddenly slide and collide. 'Slip, slip, bang' as two of them crashed to the floor. Toby himself with banana skins beneath both of his shoes then found both of his feet sliding apart.

A nearby student exclaimed, "look everyone Toby's doing the 'banana splits'!" The dinner hall became filled with laughter and amazement. Dinner supervisors who also rushed to the scene , inadvertently ended up slipping and sliding amongst the Uptown Boys who lay in defeat. There was surely a lot of correcting and cleaning to fulfil, yet at least this time both Jesse and Daz had the last laugh.

Chapter Three

Upon yawning the next morning, Jesse awoke with a smile, his entire face beaming with sheer delight. He had ventured by night to a land of dreams and had gracefully been returned back home before the new dawn.

Although he still had monumental mountains to climb, he had faced giants and was feeling more self-assured. He began to recognise that the previous instances with the Uptown Boys were not the be-all end-all. He for once could look beyond such concepts and realise he needn't be defined by temporary circumstances. For future events he would face those head on, he was going to make the best of each situation as it came.

When he returned to school in real-time, the general atmosphere had an air of pleasantry and morale was up. It would not equate to seeing the last of the Uptown Boys, but for now they seemed too busy licking their wounds. He stayed out of their way and they stayed out of his. For now he didn't need to create any banana drama!

A more fulfilled school day saw Jesse walking home with more of a spring in each step. As he approached the front garden of his home he came to notice, as though they had never been, a colourful array of rose buds displayed. His mother had planted them along with a startling set of garden gnomes to visually enhance the garden. The simple elements that he may have taken for granted now appeared as momentary bliss.

"Welcome home son." Suzie said.

"Hiya mum, your flowers look lovely!" Jesse astonishingly rushed to greet his mother with a warm tender hug, of which he had not done in years. Suzie responded with avid affection, embracing her beloved son as though cradled from birth.

"I'm so glad you like the roses, they were a present from your father, although he wouldn't actually plant them himself!" Suzie recalled.

"Glad, yeah glad indeed!" Jesse insisted.

Jesses mother, nurturing by nature, was well known for bringing a ray of sunshine to the home as well as anywhere she went. She always took the joy with her, in spite of humble beginnings, trying circumstances and unresolved issues. Perhaps a dose of this abounding joy was what Jesse needed as part of the foundation of his life.

At this time his father, although present, was still distant. His evening besides the family meal would now consist of plugging away at his 'home-work' on the laptop. Still yet to establish work-life balance, he felt the utmost importance of staring at the electronic screen for hours on end. He had to check upon his latest business transactions and stock market trading alerts.

Quality and personal time actually spent with the family would for now need to take a back seat, for he was on a mission. Yet Jesse was indeed glad that he now had Glad on his side, as a recurring remedy to help assist his unresolved situations.

By nightfall as he retreated to his bed, he was paid a visit by his fellow friend with a friendly 'rat,tat,tat,tat'. With dazzling dust at the ready they were all set to be transported to the desired land of dreams just a 'star-throw' away.

Stand and behold things are not as they seem

As you enter the world of the ever-changing dream

Tales ever captured, summoned to be told

Lessons to be learned, mysteries unfold

A meeting of the mind, sail upon the shore

A journey to be ventured, ever filled with awe

Puzzles of amazement, one shall so discern

Rise above the fear and so you may return

Through the twirling tunnel they went, mysterious creatures in view, only this time there was a mad monkey munching on a banana. He then slid away on the remaining banana skin to their sheer delight. As the bright light illuminated they were at the tunnels end. The bright light faded, yet they were now downstairs in the lounge amongst his parents. Now that very evening was now a dream evening, with a purpose to fulfil.

With Glad by his side, he would now assist by injecting food for thought. "Be fearless mi lad, with this yer dazzling dust it's high time we discuss what ye desires the most from ye mother and father." Glad said.

"Time, not just any time, but good family time, you know like we used to. We'd sit and talk for hours and play board games and stuff. Especially my father, he used to take me places you know, lots of days out. I miss the games of football we used to have!"

"No time like this weekend mi lad, what would ye like to arrange?"

"Well, there's an open 5 a side match this Saturday. I wish we could both go and even be on the same team, all ages you know. Daz is already going with his father."

"Go on, give em a sprinkling mi lad!"

Jesse inched forward and sprinkled the dust over his parents, who were seated on the couch. He then sat down on the armchair next to them, whilst they were fixated at a current argument acted out on the screen. With the dust now settled, Jesse was imminently to be dazzled by his father's suggestions.

"Hey son, I'm actually not working this weekend, how about we take a trip somewhere. Did you have anything in mind?" Jimmy said.

"Er, er, ummm, there's actually a game of footie this Saturday, everyone can bring their dad's you know."

"That's settled, a great game of footie this Saturday…….just like we used to son. Actually, there's a match on now, we could watch that if your mum doesn't mind!"

"Of course not, go ahead. I was actually thinking of baking some cookies this evening, perhaps I'll make a start now." Suzie said, grinning with bright expression. Suzie was very proficient with baking and would often bake special treats for community as well as charity events.

The evening was unfolding in nostalgic ways, very reminiscent of his earlier childhood, when quality time was part and parcel to his upbringing. The family would often go on sunny trips to the seaside as well as camping adventures in forest resorts. Theme parks were a family favourite, which usually saw both father and son screaming joyfully on roller coasters and his mother clicking away at the camera. What he would give to rekindle those times, those moments to be captured.

Although the family were not in a position to dine at restaurants on site, his mother would always bring their own essentials and pack a hearty lunch. Their lunch carry-case would be filled with sandwiches with a wide range of fillings, iced drinks, magic muffins and miniature baked treats galore. Not only would his mother pack wipes and anti-bacterial spray for the journey, but she would still personally hand him wipes after eating, often to his embarrassment.

The cookies of promise were now baked and left on a fresh tray to cool, yet they each couldn't resist a quick bite to put the taste to the test. "Wow mum, these taste exceedingly fabulous!" Jesse said, whilst helping himself to a further piece. His father soon became all smiles and was becoming more delightful by the minute.

As a surprize change of routine, the family decided upon a board game and seated themselves around the lower table on the carpet by the fireplace. This particular game involved exchanging money for goods and services, as well as winning prizes. During the heated game his father had won a new car, in which Suzie probed him with a question.

"So if you did win a new car in real-life, what would you do with it?"

"Seriously…..well as I'm already fond of the car I do have, I'd part-exchange it for a cash sum and that would go to you my son!"

"Really dad, would you?" Jesse asked enthusiastically.

"Yes, partly to invest in your further education, but as for the rest you could treat yourself with whatever you like."

"I'll hold you to that dad!" Jesse laughed.

The evening's game continued flamboyantly, in which it also got Jesse pondering as to what choices he would make if he had a lump sum of money to spend. Jesse came to appreciate that for the first time in a number of years his father took the time to personally spend with his family outside of work. The laptop was switched off, in which his mobile was even put on silent. His father had actually chosen not to entertain business calls that evening, which was a change in comparison to the usual stream of business calls. There were to be no further interruptions that evening, only to fetch the cooled cookies, so they could enjoy them by the fireplace.

A nurturing and positive home-life would surely be enhancing and beneficial to the other areas of his life, especially with school. This was now becoming his time to laugh, capture the joy and to really start to enjoy the journey. Over the up and coming days and nights he would continue to piece together the remaining pieces of his current puzzle and gain more clarity within himself.

As the night was set to fall, wishes and all, he continued to journey with Glad to the land of dreams, to a place of endless possibilities. Glad and Jesse arrived once again at Rodrum Academy, all set for the day ahead. Their first point of call was a period of Drama, which was a class held by Mr Shrink who helped his students to grow. After the initial registration, he assembled the pupils into smaller groups, although not of their personal choosing.

As was common practice with this particular class, a handful of the pupils were non-compliant with the instructions, as they were unhappy with their choice. This also demonstrated that Jesse was not the only 'target' in this class, in which a few of the other pupils would at times endure unpleasant instances.

Disapproval of the choices was then boldly declared by one of the Uptown Boys. "I will not be in the same group as him, her, him and especially him!"

"Well, that is not your choice to make!" Mr Shrink recalled.

"Sorry sir, but this one, well he has a big nose that doesn't quite agree with me!" He then pointed with his finger. "I'm just hoping that one day it will simply shrink, er sorry Mr Shrink!"

"Still not your choice, we will continue with the groups exactly as you have been assigned. Also in future any inappropriate comments will see students designated the relevant detention – YOU HAVE BEEN WARNED. In this school we are to treat each other with manners and respect."

Each group had to create a role play performance based on any of the works of Shakespeare. Towards the later part of the lesson a few of the groups would be given an opportunity to act out their short play in front of the rest of the class. At this point they sat as an audience to the performing group on rows of aligned benches.

Jesse found himself beneficially placed in the row exactly behind the pupil who had generated all the fuss. Jesse knew this was his moment to sprinkle his dazzling dust upon the disruptive pupil, so as to enable him to learn a lesson for once.

As the dazzling dust went to work Jesse decided that this pupil's nose would be the main object on show. A second group had now been selected to perform which included the pupil who was dust unaware. It was now a few minutes into the performance and it was the turn of this pupil to voice his lines. As he began to speak he suddenly came to a halt. 'Scratch, scratch, scratch'. "Er sorry, one moment, my nose has suddenly really decided to itch." The itching then paused for a while and he then felt free to continue.

Moments later as his line came up, his nose began to bother him again......really bother him. He now felt he couldn't continue. He then distressingly reached into his pocket and took out his only tissue. He then proceeded to blow his nose to try to remedy the fact that it was now running. All of his trying solutions were to no avail.

Not only did his nose continue to run, but his tissue decided to fly, fly away. He quickly ran after the tissue, whilst scratching and scratching. He soon became so irate and disturbed that the only solution was to run and hind behind the dark curtain screen at the end of the room.

As he sat shivering and sniffling in hiding, the only replacement for the tissue he required was the use of one of his socks. Not the prettiest sight, but he hastily removed his left shoe and utilised his sock as a tissue. He really needed to blow his nose and SNEEZE. Finally all the itching had stopped, however now upon looking up realised that the whole class was now staring at him. This indeed was not one of his finer moments.

"Well done mi lad." Glad sang in a cinematic tone. "I must say ye has certainly taught him a lesson or two. Time for the next lesson in the history block, let's be on our way mi lad."

As the pupils aligned for their history lesson, a number of the pupils decided to try and squeeze all at once through the slim line doorway. For some pupils, patience was not their virtue, in which the 'caffufle' continued for some time. The pupils eventually made their way to their respective seats, whereby the objectives of the lesson were soon to be summarised by the class teacher Miss Tiny.

On a number of occasions a few of the more personally inquisitive pupils would question Miss Tiny as to why she was not yet a Mrs. "Miss Tiny, er why are you not married yet and when are you going to be?" One of the seated pupils enquired.

"Thank you, but that is a personal question and we have already discussed beforehand, that personal questions to teachers are out of bounds." She then proceeded to commence the lesson activities as planned.

"Er miss, have, have you got any pets, a mouse or a Rottweiler perhaps." Another pupil asked. The class of pupils soon burst into laughter.

"ENOUGH, such a question is irrelevant for the day ahead, so let's continue. Now if you could all carry on with your presentation sheets in your green folders." The pupils were each working on the preparations for conducting their presentations in turn, in front of the class.

The theme of the presentations was historical figures in history, in which they were to elaborate on noble acts that such figures had accomplished. Whilst Jesse's choice of personalities was Napoleon, Daz had chosen Christopher Columbus. A few of the Uptown Boys were requested to amend their selected choices as Frankenstein and Bambi would just not do.

Towards the second half of the lesson, three of the pupils were to be chosen at random to present their work in front of the class. The first pupil of which had chosen President Roosevelt, was a shining example to the others and had carried out his presentation remarkably.

The second and third pupils in line were pre-advised that their presentations would soon follow. The third pupil due to present was indeed Toby, who appeared to sit with a nervous disposition. As he was quite a distance from Jesse's seat, he wasn't close enough to dazzle him with his dust. As Glad was more than glad to be of service, he would on this occasion assist him with the dusting.

With quiet operation Jesse managed to open the jar beneath his desk and hand a portion of the dust to Glad's open hand. In a humorous manner, as the class would be unaware of his presence, he then danced quirkily over to Toby. 'Sprinkle, sprinkle, sprinkle' and so the dust was now covering Toby. Jesse was all too aware of his dazzling plan for Toby and he continued to be seated calmly to await the ensuing entertainment.

The ultimate time had come for a very shaky Toby to present his historical masterpiece to the class. His presentation would also involve writing on the white board with the inclusion of a diagram as well as text. His chosen figure had been changed to Elizabeth I, yet he had not allotted adequate time in which to conduct his research. He began with a brief overview of the life of Elizabeth I and he shortly made his way to the whiteboard to then present.

As Toby had his written notes to hand, he was fully aware of the sentences and diagram that he wanted to include. As the dazzling dust was carrying out its own assignment, the whiteboard pen was now going to have a mind of its own. Toby began to piece together the words of his first sentence, which should have been about Elizabeth I. As the pen moved it wrote 'I am a jolly big pig who likes to roll around in the mud.'

The teacher became flabbergasted, whilst the pupils with roars of laughter were both shocked and amazed. Was this really the research that he had took the time to create? Did this really reflect the purpose of the assignment? Well according to the marker pen it did.

Toby himself was taken aback and then quickly erased the inappropriate sentence. He then attempted to write another sentence. On this occasion it read 'I like to swim after the gym and my yellow teeth really like to grin'. The class was now beyond amazement and disorder had commenced.

"It's not me miss, it's the pen, it's writing its own words." Toby pleaded.

"Do you really expect me to believe that Toby. Well since you are choosing not to write in an appropriate manner, can you now get on with your diagram?" Miss Tiny asked in an annoyed manner.

The class sat now in utter silence, whilst contemplating what type of diagram Toby would invent. His specific aim was to draw a figure of Elizabeth I seated on her throne. As the pen made contact with the board, the drawing soon became a comical caricature of Miss Tiny. She was drawn with a combination of bulging eyes, whiskers, rabbit teeth, a droopy chin, oversized spectacles and a giant round left foot. What on planet Earth was Toby thinking of?

A very irate Miss Tiny then said furiously, "TOBY, I'VE HAD MORE THAN ENOUGH OF YOUR JOKES. FIRST DETENTION IS SET FOR YOU AND YOU CAN NOW GO STRAIGHT TO THE HEADMASTER'S OFFICE."

A rather baffled and confused Toby walked slowly, with slumped shoulders, down the corridor on his way to the 'door of doom'. What was actually a short trip, now felt like a lifetime. He really could not fathom how an ordinary marker pen could play such unwholesome tricks on him. Furthermore, he could not comprehend why he was having such a disruptive week. He felt as though his personal world had changed axis and was turning upside down.

The 'door of doom' was near approaching and was drawing closer and closer. As he stood directly in front of the door he couldn't help but scratch his head in bewilderment, he felt unable to unscramble his thoughts. In a blurry daze he then began to hear strange voices in his head, whispering and repeating utterances of reprimand. 'You've been a very bad boy Toby, ooooh Toby. You've had a bad week Toby. What you have done to others will come back to you ooooh Toby.' The voices soon began to fade into the background and he suddenly felt the desire to clean his ears with the use of his fingers.

He knocked several times on the headmaster's door and a stern voice called, "come in". As the door opened slowly and the gap began to widen, the hinge of the door began to creek. Toby then edged slowly in small steps towards the headmaster at his desk. Mr Wary had a fixed glare towards Toby, which the pupils were used to for many a lengthened year.

"Good day Toby, can you explain why you have been sent to my office.......again." Mr Wary asked.

"I, I, I, had a problem with the marker pen when I was doing my presentation sir."

"A problem, what sort of problem?"

"Well, the pen you see was not writing what I wanted it to write. Sir, it was writing its own words." Toby recalled.

"We what other words was your pen writing Toby?"

"Erm, words like 'I'm a big pig' and stuff, but it wasn't me sir, it was the pen, it's the truth!"   Toby insisted.

At this moment, with Toby very wary of him, Mr Wary let out a huge sigh and exclaimed. "Toby, I have for some time held you in high regard, as by now I thought you had corrected your ways. However you are back here in my office with continued spells of trouble. As well as detention Toby, I have no choice but to advise your parents of your recent behaviour!"

"No, please don't sir, I won't do it again!" Toby pleaded.

"It's settled, your parents will be informed accordingly, now please make your way back to class, you are dismissed." Mr Wary said.

The days were now unfolding very brightly for both Jesse and Glad,

however their rivals were experiencing a mixture of undesirable events.

Chapter Four

It was another bright and dazzling day in the land of dreams and Toby's class were busy with the preparations for their assembly later that morning. The assembly was to be performed to all of the other classes in the year group. The assembly theme was animals, in which they had three real-life animals brought in for illustrative purposes. Two hamsters and a rabbit were all included, whilst waiting calmly in their respective compartments.

The eager pupils were all excited for their informative assembly, whereby they would elaborate on varied aspects and roles of a number of animals. The form teacher Mrs Robbins had assembled a small group of well mannered pupils to supervise and carry the animals in line towards the assembly.

The class proceeded in due formation and arrived at the school hall. The other classes along with their form teachers were patiently seated, ready for the assembly to commence. With animals in tow, the class positioned themselves in alignment on the benches that were laid out at the front of the hall. There were three additional chairs situated further in front, in which three pupils as well as the animals would later be seated.

Glad insisted that Jesse seat himself on the bench just behind Toby, just in case he had a reason to bring out the dust. The opening part included a brief introduction by two cheerful and promising pupils. A selection of pupils then presented posters with their corresponding scripts of detailed facts about a number of the animals. An array of animals including horses, guinea pigs, frogs, rats, small insects and grasshoppers.

Despite being given the benefit of the doubt, Toby began his 'uncalled-for' acts and turned around to intimidate Jesse with cold looks and unkind words. Glad encouraged Jesse to not provide him with a reaction and to sprinkle the dust at the next available moment.

With the assembly in full swing, Jesse then took the opportunity to dust him off again and paused for creative thought. As a chance to demonstrate more desirable behaviour, Toby was chosen along with two other pupils to sit with the animals on the three chairs.

A few supervisory pupils were on hand to assist with the animals. The two hamsters were each to remain in their respective compartments, whilst the rabbit was permitted to sit calmly on the lap of Toby. Although Jesse knew what would soon follow, Toby was blissfully unaware.

As the seating arrangements were in place, a short talk was given by a few of the pupils, to enlighten the classes on hamsters and rabbits. The presentation which would go on for several minutes was well received, with due applause.

To the utter amazement of the crowd, a muddled mass of rabbit droppings were strewn all over Toby's lap. As the rabbit was lifted and removed, Toby yelled out in shock horror. "Aaaargh, droppings miss, it's everywhere!" The audience laughed hysterically as Toby stood up at once. He felt that he had no choice but to run off and leave the assembly in quick succession. A very amused teacher ran out after him, so as to be of further assistance. Both Jesse and Glad were highly chuckled as the day for them had really only just begun.

For as long as it took, they would have more dust in store. Jesse held onto the hope that one day Toby and his friends would realise that their unacceptable ways were no longer going to be tolerated.

After the lunch hour Jesse checked once again to ensure that he had fully packed his swimming trunks, cap and goggles. He zipped his bag up firmly and hoisted it on to his back, as he joined the queue for the coach.

Jesse highly enjoyed school swimming visits, as one step on the coach always brought back fond memories of previous coach trips with his family. On such school visits there was to be no eating on the coach, although a few of the pupils would have a small stash of snacks in their coat pockets to enjoy. Any such snacks that were discovered were instantaneously confiscated. The collection of those snacks were then hidden away in the top draw of Mrs Robbins desk. On occasions when Mrs Robbins was waylaid with book marking she had an untold tendency to dip into the snacks and eat one, or two, or three!

The class arrived surely and safely at the swimming centre and made their way into two lines. They proceeded to their separate changing areas to prepare for the lesson ahead. Every other week would usually see at least one pupil miss the swimming lesson, as a consequence of leaving their required kits at home.

The majority of pupils took no time at all to change into their kits, yet there were always the few who got changed at snail pace. Such a pace gave Jesse a useful moment to sprinkle his dust over Toby whilst strolling past him.

As the class was aligned by the baths ready for instruction, Jesse re-positioned his goggles. The class then adhered to listen to the swimming instructor, who began with advising them on health and safety aspects. Whilst beginners were situated in the shallow pool, the more proficient pupils made their way to the adjacent deeper pool. Both Jesse and Toby were in the group for the shallow pool.

With the assistance of the dust Jesse decided that Toby was not going to be as bold and confident to step into the shallow waters. The pupils were then calmly asked in turn to go into the water by the instructor. Upon Jesse's turn, he confidently climbed down and awaited the turn of the other pupils in a merrily manner.

It was imminently coming to Toby's turn, however it wasn't just the pupils in the water that caught Toby's eye. Suddenly and with sheer surprise, Toby noticed slithery fish swimming in the water. To his astonishment he then became aware of flipping salmon in all manner of directions. As if this wasn't enough he then noticed two dolphins in this strange pool. He instantly hoped that he would not now come across even larger creatures with jaws.

As the instructor instructed him to enter the pool, he yelled at once.

"Noooo, I can't go in, there's fish, there's fish I tell you!"

"Actually there are no fish, only pupils, so can you now please make your way into the water." The instructor replied.

"Look, look, there's a dolphin, I refuuuuuuse to go into that pool!" Once again his classmates responded with bursts of laughter as they couldn't figure out the validity of his excuses. Toby continued to plead his case and refused to go into the pool. He then found himself duly dismissed, whilst the remainder of the pupils resumed their lesson.

During the returning journey back to school, a number of the pupils decided to create a song to mark the magical moment.

Fish, fish, I think he's seen a fish

If we all just carry on

He might just get his wish

Pool, pool, he won't go in the pool

He has chose not to obey

He won't observe the rule

Leave, leave, I think he wants to leave

The pool is always very clear

He just will not believe

Stare, stare, I cannot help but stare

He has seen a dolphin there

But we are not aware

Whilst a number of pupils had damp hair, Toby was assuredly dry, as he had on this occasion chosen not to partake. Even his closest friends were beginning to feel confused as to his inner state.

The up and coming weekend was still two days away, yet he didn't have that Friday feeling of a fun-filled school day to come. Glad had happily followed Jesse back home to his mother's welcoming outstretched arms. Suzie, always of a friendly disposition, was becoming more cheery by the day. She was simply delighted that the bond between her and Jesse had rekindled with blossoming force. Jesse now looked forward to his snacks and now had the habit of initiating designated time for his homework.

During his television time, he was however, very fixated on programmes that included superheroes. The idea of someone more powerful who could provide everyday solutions quite intrigued him. In many ways Glad himself was a personal superhero to him. He had assisted him with unresolved situations and was additionally helping him to embrace his identity.

The evening was approaching and Jimmy had returned home, yet earlier than usual. For the last few days he was on a renewed mission to make family time a bigger priority. His mother was finishing her preparations to make vegetable soup for tea, along with tasty bakes that she had prepared earlier.

In times gone by when Jesse's parents had first met, Suzie had been working as a secretary for a major corporation. Her role involved working from dusk till dawn, with her Sundays free. Suzie worked amongst a talented pool of acquaintances, as well as business moguls.

Although she was competent at her role and managed to meet her ensuing deadlines, she was seeking a greater work-life balance. She initially approached her boss to seek a part-time schedule, yet such a high-flying 'winner' was not willing to re-arrange.

In time she happily became married to Jimmy and between them it was agreed that he would help her begin her own business from home. Although her co-workers were sad to see her move on, she was now willing to embrace new opportunities on the horizon. Suzie had a useful range of transitional skills, as well as multi-tasking ability. On the other hand Jimmy was well acquainted with business enterprise and product promotion.

The two lovebirds entwined their thoughts and so brought together their business ideas. He assisted her with all the necessary tools to bring her ideas to life and to begin her business venture. To this day her online company is prospering in motion and enables her to be flexible with her time. Her new role has enabled her to invest both time in her business, yet also precious time with her family.

Whilst the soup was simmering yet on a high heat, unbeknown to Suzie, the family challenged each other to a game of cards. Such beloved time was becoming more frequent and meaningful conversation was becoming more established. They soon began to discuss the very excursions that they would plan to take over the remaining year.

Coach trips, countryside retreats, beach resorts and landscape bike rides were all on the agenda. As family trips were so dear to Jesse, he could recall at the drop of a hat the splendid occasions he had experienced. He could to this day still taste the delicious chocolate that he tried at the factory, he could still hear the rush of the waves on the ferry trips he took. He realised now that as a family, they were about to embark on precious adventures once again, all of which he so longed for.

The very concept that he was beginning to embrace from his mother, was to make the best of everything. She would make an avid count of her blessings, instead of her problems. Suzie would always seek the sunshine in all situations, even on dark cold nights.

The family whilst being entertained were so enraptured in their activity, that it was not realised that the soup was now bubbling over. As the bubbles could now be heard in full effect, Jimmy called out. "The pot is bubbling up and bubbling up!" Suzie quickly rushed to the scene and calmed the heat, whilst sprinkling a dash of cool water from a cup over the soup.

With the soup now savoured, the family went on to enjoy a delicious meal and continue their conversations. In a brief moment Jesse had realised that the bubbling soup had sparked an idea for his next chemistry lesson. As the up and coming lesson would entail the mixing of liquid elements, he could now ensure that Toby would have a bubbling time.

The evening had gone by and Jesse well accompanied by Glad was getting ready to enter the land of dreams.

Stand and behold things are not as they seem

As you enter the world of the ever-changing dream

Tales ever captured, summoned to be told

Lessons to be learned, mysteries unfold

A meeting of the mind, sail upon the shore

A journey to be ventured, ever filled with awe

Puzzles of amazement, one shall so discern

Rise above the fear and so you may return

As the pearly purple gates came into view, Jesse was soon accompanied by Daz and they made their way up the path. "Hope you've still memorized the periodic table, our science test is next week!" Daz said.

"Oh yeah, will do, I'll get round to it!" Jesse answered. At this present moment scientific knowledge was not the only item on the agenda.

Jesse, Daz, Glad and the dazzling dust made their way to the science block. In the chemistry room as there were a number of practical displays situated around the room, pupils were often asked to stop fiddling with displayed items.

The chemistry teacher, Mr Muddows had spent the earlier part of the morning preparing for the practical lesson ahead. On many occasions this also meant that he could not always make it to the teacher's meetings before the start of school.

Mr Muddows gave an overview of the chemicals they would be mixing and advised them to be aware of any substance that may be hot. Mr Muddows who had arranged the class to sit in pairs, went around the room to provide them with their task sheets. According to one pupil, given substances were not the only things that could be deemed hot.

"Ew sir, do you mind removing your hot breath!"

"I beg your pardon!" Mr Muddows responded.

"Breath sir, it's very hot, very hot indeed!"

"Warning number one, any further inappropriate comments and you'll be reprimanded accordingly." Mr Muddows said.

The practical experiments were now underway, in which pupils would at times visit the sink area to dispense of used chemicals. In the far corner Toby had decided to offer Jesse a cold look and additionally began making ludicrous faces. A while later, as Toby made his way to the sink area, Jesse followed on with dazzling dust at the ready. The sprinkling had been accomplished and a dazzling event was yet to come.

Each pair continued to conduct their practical experiments, taking turns as required. Toby with his chemistry partner on standby, began to measure a clear chemical substance, of which he mixed with a teaspoon of powder. The desired result was for the substance to simply change colour. All of a sudden bubbles began to rise to the surface, followed by a louder host of bubbles. The substance then began to rise and ooze over, spilling out onto the table. Loud bubbles then began popping sporadically causing a sudden frenzy. "Toby, what on Earth is going on here!" Mr Muddows shrieked.

"Er, sir it just started bubbling over, I don't know why!" Toby exclaimed.

The pairs of pupils stood baffled in amazement, as to why this pair's experiment was the only one to go wild. It took several further attempts, with all hands on deck to rectify the situation. What made matters worse is that school inspectors who were visiting a range of classes to check on school progress, were now at the door. As they stood at the open door, the view consisted of a vast array of paper towels splattered over the surfaces, a soaking wet soapy floor and a very drenched overall worn by Toby. Not the most organised display, but Mr Muddows would now have to make do with the existing presentation.

Although seemingly composed on the outside, Jesse was pretty much having a whale of a time on the inside. Toby was still yet to transform his conduct, which is why the dust was still required.

Chapter Five

Saturday mornings would usually consist of helping his mother with dusting and polishing so as to earn extra pocket money. Jesse would then pay full attention to his computer games, before heading to the shops to spend his earned keep.

On this day, as he rubbed his eyes, he was still readjusting to real-time as he had recently returned from the land of dreams. "Jesse still getting ready for the footie?" Jimmy enquired.

"Huh", mumbled Jesse.

"The footie Jesse it's today!"

"Oh yeah dad, I'm just getting ready". Jesse assured.

He then remembered his father's promise for today, which would fundamentally be a father and son day. By the time Jesse arrived downstairs his breakfast awaited him at the table, courtesy of his cheerful mother. Suzie always chose to assemble the cutlery in restaurant fashion along with creatively displayed napkins. On the inside she was a queen and this was her castle.

Jesse enjoyed his bowl of Sunny Pops, a piece of wholemeal toast, chopped bananas for energy and a glass of freshly squeezed juice. He was all set for the day ahead and so was his father. His father was seated in a pleasant manner, whilst enjoying a bowl of oatmeal topped with berries.

No sooner did he finish and his mother was on hand with her marigolds to clear the table. In a surprisingly helpful mood, she was then brought to a standstill by Jimmy, who decided that he was going to where the rubber gloves, clear the table and do the dishes.

"Relax dear, the gloves are on me!" Jimmy advised. Whilst scrubbing away at the dishes, he was seconds away from dropping a dish on the floor, but managed to catch it in time. "Practice makes perfect!" Jimmy said.

It was not long now till they were off to play football and Jimmy was loading the bags into the boot of the car. Jesse did always prefer his father's sturdy silver car and liked to arrive in style in this vehicle. En route to the match they drove through picturesque villages and both couldn't resist shouting 'wee' as they went over the hill of a bridge. It was very reflective of former times, in which the day would have its own natural sparkle.

As they arrived at the grounds, a number of families had already arrived, with eager participants carrying out their personal warm-ups. Young players could be seen jumping up and down, whilst their respective fathers did stretching, as well as soothing their joints.

One or two fathers felt the need to loudly huff and puff so as to display their dominance. The club official made his way to the centre of the pitch and gathered all participants together. The relevant teams were organised, in which Jesse and his father were allocated in the second team, playing on pitch three. Each pitch was individually refereed and team captains assigned.

With the players poised for action, the match was set in motion. The gleaming sun duly brightened the morning sky, as intense faces watched by. Players dodged to the left and right and honed their tactical skills. Jesse was both a fan of the sport as well an avid team player. He was simultaneously on the lookout for open opportunities to pass the ball to his father. Jimmy had so far managed to dribble the ball, albeit for a few glorified seconds. He was catching on to the team spirit and enthusiastically embraced the game.

By the second half of the game they were both down by one more point, in which the score board read as 2:1. Although Jesse was not a bad loser and would ordinarily demonstrate good sportsmanship, he wanted his father to be on the winning team.

In the flicker of a moment the ball was passed directly to Jesse, another player had rushed in to tackle the ball. Jesse swerved sideways, in which the opposing player quickly stretched his foot outwards. Jesse instantly tripped over his leg, whilst being forcibly pushed to the ground by his opponent. There was a loud thump as he fell to the ground. The referee who had witnessed the brief assault, hurriedly rushed to his side.

"That was a deliberate push, I saw it." One of Jesse's team mates yelled.

Jesse rapidly rubbed the area of his leg that was in a slight degree of discomfort. As his father came over to tend to his son, Jesse insisted. "I'll be alright, let's get back to the game." Just then his father ruffled Jesse's hair with his hand and said. "That's my lad, I'm so proud of you!" Jesse had longed to hear such a profound statement, especially coming from his father.

It was fairly decided that Jesse's team be awarded a penalty, which had gladdening appeal for his team mates. Jesse looked on towards the goal, with a solid stance, as he positioned himself to take the penalty. His surroundings were filled with seconds of silence as he paused for his momentous moment. As he gravitated forward he took a bold shot, the ball soared across the pitch, to the back of the net. The crowd went wild with continued acclamation, a victorious moment indeed.

The challenge continued, but any further goal was still yet to be scored. They were now three minutes from the end of the match and the general morale was waning. Jesse may not have had his dust to dazzle the game with, but he trusted in his personal ability and his desire to succeed. Jesse soon caught sight of his father with the ball at his feet,

who had also become aware of Jesse in an open zone. Jesse was
eyeing up his father with all readiness.

Jimmy gracefully passed the ball to Jesse, who took on the challenge
with no hesitation. He dribbled the ball, he dodged the players in view,
they were merely seconds until countdown. The goalie was shifting in
position, set to defend, aiming to block. Jesse took the final shot and in
the final countdown - he scored. "Yeah, yeah, we've won". Another
team mate exclaimed. As the crowds cheered Jesse became joyfully
surrounded by the other players. His father took a bold step and picked
Jesse up with both arms, lifting up his personal champion. Jesse was
thrilled with excitement and was surely glad.

On the journey back home, both Jimmy and Jesse were grinning with
enthusiasm. The day had unfolded tremendously and Jesse had began
to realise that it would be a great opportunity to play football more. He
wasn't yet on the school team and his family were not yet able to
purchase the required full kit along with trendy football boots. He
thought to himself however that surely one day this desire could be
fulfilled. If he was wholeheartedly willing enough, surely there had to be

a way. "One of these days, we'll get you on the school team, my lad - one day!" Jimmy said.

"Yeah, that would be awesome." Jesse replied.

En route to their destination they stopped at a local petrol station. Although this was not a visit for petrol, Jimmy decided that they both could browse through the magazines on sale. Jesse was instantly drawn to the football magazines on display. "Choose any two magazines that you like my lad." Jimmy said. Jesse had already decided upon his choice in his mind and so picked up the two magazines that appealed to him.

The two skilful players arrived back home, eager to share their news. As his mother looked on at them in the hallway, both Jimmy and Jesse were telling her the news at the same time. Neither could get a louder word in edgeways. Yet before she could receive their verbal offerings, she took a glaring eye at their muddy boots to imply that they should be removed. With the dirt kept at the door, they made their way inside and delighted Suzie with their accomplishments. "Star of the day he is, star of the day!" Jimmy mentioned.

They each got themselves ready, as lunch was being prepared, as Suzie was elated to be once again in the company of her two stars. Shortly after lunch Suzie spontaneously decided that she was going to make pancakes, with the keen assistance of Jesse. "Making pancakes mum, but it's not Shrove Tuesday!" Jesse stated ironically.

"Well romance shouldn't be just celebrated on Valentine's day, appreciation of one's life shouldn't be limited to birthdays and if it is on my mind to feast on pancakes, that can be any day also!" Suzie declared.

Off to the kitchen she went with shiny aprons at the ready. Suzie along with her organisational skills had laid out all her ingredients, equipment and cookware. Jesse just needed to present himself and crack on with the mixing. Suzie always liked the mixture to be of a refined texture and ensured that Jesse whisked the flour and milk thoroughly. As the mixture poured into the pre-heated pan, it was then set on a low heat. After several minutes, then came the time to carry out the famous 'flipping'. Jesse carefully held up the pan, with his mother on standby and tossed it like a tossed coin. The pancake was then left for several more minutes before being served on dishes. To add flare to their delightful dessert, the pancakes were cut into heart shapes, decorated with berries and a special chocolate dust. The pancakes went down a treat and were enjoyed by all.

By mid afternoon, as the weather was still bright, Jimmy and Jesse went for a relaxing bike ride towards the local valley. Situated by the valley was a popular park which had been regenerated. The area now boasted a modernised lake, equipped with paddling boats, an outdoor gym, horse stables, an assault course and blossoming gardens.

On this occasion, they were simply going to ride through the idyllic area, with his father's promise that they would return again to enjoy the other activities. As they rode by, there was an array of families who were spending quality time relishing the outdoor activities and the fine weather. The main activity that Jesse was keen to try was the assault course. This recreational facility included a rock climbing section, as well as a fairly high zip-wire. As Jesse was not so fond of heights, it would be a 'sure-fire' challenge for him, but he was all set to overcome.

Chapter Six

The Jobson family were enjoying a blissful evening as they watched a television game show. Contestants were quizzed with questions of general knowledge as well as popular topics including sport, history, music, literature and the like. For shows like these, the Jobson family could often be heard calling out the answers, in which sound proof walls would come in handy.

"How could you get that answer wrong, just how could you not know that, are you crazy?" Jimmy yelled towards the current contestant on the screen.

"He can't hear you, you know and by the way, it's just a game show, it's not real-life!" Suzie indicated.

Jimmy was well known for taking both game shows as well as the dramas acted out in popular soaps, quite seriously. If there was an issue he could identify with, it meant real-life for him, in which he would often become engrossed in the plot. Suzie even hinted the suggestion that since he was so emotionally involved in television series, he should try and become an actor himself.

Jimmy was now becoming very heated and before the conclusion of the final round, there was an unforeseen blackout. There had been an electrical fault in the local area, which meant it was lights out! Jimmy with his mobile phone to hand, switched on the lamp of his device. Suzie then did the same, in which the family continued sitting.

"Don't worry now, I'm sure they'll be fixing the fault very soon, at least we have each other!" Suzie insisted. The three of them then huddled together closely, until the lights subsequently came back on.

"Brush teeth and bed me thinks!" Suzie said to Jesse, who was now feeling rather sleepy. Jesse dutifully climbed up the stairs and got himself ready for bed.

Jesse had quietly rested for some time, in which he had kept his night lamp on to add to the soothing surroundings.

'Tap,tap,tap', came the knocks at the door and so his peaceful tranquillity was no longer. As the fluorescent green light appeared, Glad had once again come into being. "Good evening mi lad, it seems as though one has thoroughly enjoyed a jolly weekend."

"Good evening Glad, just two minutes more sleep and I'll be with you!" Jesse slurred.

"Ah ha, we can enjoy plenty more minutes in the land of dreams mi lad, let's be on our way!" Glad insisted.

As Jesse arose he tossed his pillow aside and stepped alongside Glad. As Glad embraced his arm, he chanted his endearing verse. They disappeared from view only to appear at the entrance of Rodrum Academy.

Elizabeth was waiting at the entrance, whilst glancing down at her school diary. Although she had greeted a number of passing pupils, as Jesse walked by she did not pay him any mind. Throughout her time at school, their paths had not crossed, in which she may have vaguely known of him, but didn't really get to know him.

"See anyone you admire mi lad?" Glad quizzed Jesse and gave him a sudden wink.

"I do, but I'm not speaking to her yet. One day I will pluck up the courage to, but not today!"

"Don't worry mi lad, when that happens, I'll be right by your side!"

"Not unless it's in real-time though!" Jesse replied. Glad promptly handed Jesse a refilled jar of dazzling dust, as the moments when it would be required were so varied.

There would also be the added variety to this particular school week, as there would be a chemistry test, a trip to the local nature reserve as well as sports day. No matter how many occasions the dust would be required this week, there was certainly going to be adventure.

Jesse and Glad continued up the corridor only to see before them a confusing crowd who appeared to be causing friction. It had come to their attention that a young boy was being surrounded by a group of bothersome pupils who were trying to humiliate him for the style of his glasses. As his prescribed thick glasses were not deemed fashionable by the group, they sought to highlight apparent differences.

"They're so wide I could swim in those glasses!" One of them called out.

"Yeah, large enough to host the Olympics!" Another replied.

Jesse did not feel pleased at such an event and decided it was time for him to help assist with the matter himself. As he stood amongst the unruly crowd, he ensured he was within a good distance to sprinkle the dust on the majority of them. With the power of the dust he was able to create a bag full of marbles, just like a magic trick from his school bag. The marbles were quickly released to cover the surrounding floor. The very crowd who had thought that they had got the better of the defenceless pupil, were now slipping, sliding and stumbling to the ground. 'Thump, thump, thump' and down they went like retired trees. When opportunity didn't come knocking, he built his own door so that they could go tumbling.

"Ah ha, they're making spectacles of themselves!" A nearby pupil said hysterically.

The remaining pupils in the hall were buzzing with excitement. A frustrated looking teacher came rushing down the hall, like an angry dog ready to pounce.

"Just what is going on here, get up, get up and what are all these marbles doing on the floor!"

The well stood pupils, including Jesse all took this open opportunity to quickly escape from the scene. All that were left were the sorry group of pupils, struggling to rise and a disappointing teacher standing over, tapping his feet. Jesse was now on his way to becoming a fully fledged dazzler, seeking to address situations, just like the superheroes he revered.

Jesse was thankful that he went over his revision of the periodic table, even if it was left till the night before. The only concern he had about classroom tests was that an individual teacher could not always keep their eye on all pupils at all times. With the blink of an eye, a few pupils would take the opportunity to try and cheat or even exchange notes on strips of paper. This was by no means Jesse's method of conduct, as such actions would result in him only cheating himself.

Luckily for him there was a teaching assistant who had been designated to help supervise the chemistry lesson that day. This at least meant that there would be another pair of eyes on watch, especially for the likes of Toby. Toby had taken several opportunities previously to exchange notes as well as glance at the answers of nearby pupils.

The class were all seated with readiness to begin and seemed eager to get started. In a brief moment the teaching assistant advised Mr Muddows of a practical idea to adjust the seating arrangements. In doing so, pupils who would normally and secretly converse during such tests were no longer situated nearby assisting peers.

As there could be no walking around once the tests ensued, Glad was directly on hand to transfer the dust to where it needed to go. The test had begun with instructed silence, with a contented Mr Muddows working away at a sheet on his desk.

The timer on the electronic board was set, which would duly sound as the test came to a close. Fortunately for Jesse the teaching assistant had eyes like a hawk and was consistently looking around for any practical discrepancies.

As the pupils were getting on with the task at hand, Toby had created a note in an undercover manner, which he had intended to pass on to the next available candidate. Jesse quickly winced at Glad and motioned his head in the direction of Toby, so as to indicate that he required the dust. Without delay, Glad rose to the occasion and sprinkled the dust over Toby. Meanwhile Toby, little by little continued to formulate his private note. Unbeknown to Toby the note would now transform itself into a miniature paper aeroplane and go flying. Crease by crease the mysterious note began to fold, causing Toby to feel anxious and confused.

The aeroplane was in full force and was ready to launch. It raised itself higher with an equally anxious teaching assistant looking onwards. The note then embarked on its journey into the very hands of the teaching assistant. She inquisitively unfolded the aeroplane in a flash of a moment to reveal the words 'can you tell me the answer to number 5,6, and 7'.

"TOBY, STAND UP AT ONCE!" The teaching assistant exclaimed. She stormed straight over to Mr Muddows and informed him of the misconduct.

"Cheat, cheat, you think you can try and cheat. Well not round here. Okay, since you want to try and cheat, you can do your test individually during lunchtime. That way you'll have no other pupils to copy from!"

Jesse was beyond contentment at the sight of such corrections, as he didn't think cheating in general was fair and should be dealt with.

An illustrative geography lesson followed on from chemistry, with the purpose of exploring different weather systems. This particular class were both receptive and obedient in manner and got off to a flying start. The only lesson breaks consisted of the yelling coming from the opposite classroom. In that class however, were a variety of pupils, the majority were orderly in conduct, yet there were well known characters that always put on a show.

Evert ten minutes 'GET OUT', 'NOT IN MY CLASSROOM' and 'ENOUGH IS ENOUGH' would be vocalised by the teacher who had to deal with all manner of incidents. Yet another eventful day at Rodrum Academy. Quite often the sound of a slammed door of the class meant that the same characters were being sent off to the headmaster's office. As the raised voices were heard, so other heads would turn.

The dazzling dust was not required for the remainder of the school day, as there were no further untoward occurrences to disrupt the day. What was unusual however was that at particular moments throughout the day, Elizabeth began to appear to try and make eye contact with Jesse. This was certainly a first for him in the world and he steadily began to reciprocate her glances. Yet for now actual conversation felt beyond his capacity to currently establish. Perhaps on the trip to the nature reserve a relevant opportunity may come about. He now had a stream of thoughts circulating through his mind, unsure of his approach, yet certain that it had to come about.

Chapter Seven

A transfiguration of time, a change of scene, yet so it was his advancing opportunity to be courageous. To follow his dreams and to discover his capabilities. Through the twirling tunnel he now had access to chances not previously taken.

As Glad guided him through, they arrived in time to a series of double-decker buses aligned near the school gates. Jesse, as per his routine, checked through his bag once again to ensure that he had all his belongings with him, his packed lunch and his dazzling dust. His mother insisted on him bringing the colourful train lunch box that he had since primary school. He remained obedient to her wishes , as he felt in no position to change it - but one day!

The entire year group were geared up for their ling awaited trip to the nature reserve. The form tutors readily assembled the pupils into their groups and conducted the register call. With all pupils present they each in turn hopped aboard their designated buses.

Jesse was on the second bus, which meant that he was able to view the usual antics on the bus in front as well as on the bus behind. As the buses rode ahead, the comic show had begun. Pupils half seated on the bus in front could be seen smirking whilst turning around to pull faces. The buses were filled with chuckles of laughter and an atmosphere of merriment. The accompanying teachers were not always equally delighted and sought to continue responding in a monotonous tone, so as to not provoke the pupils further.

The route to the nature reserve included country roads, in which fields and farmed areas would come into view. As soon as the pupils became aware of farm animals they would bellow the corresponding animal noises to the top of their voices. 'Moo, moo, moo, baah, baah, baah.'

The teachers would feel pretty relieved as they arrived onsite to their destination. The pupils coming off the buses with all excitement made their way to their respective groups . Jesse was in the same group as Elizabeth, as if by happenstance. His form teacher Mrs Robbins was also accompanied by two teaching assistants.

"On the way to the nature reserve, you are all to keep in line." Mrs Robbins addressed the group.

The group marched on in army mode towards the main entrance. As there was a tourist gift shop on site, pupils were permitted to bring up to £5 to spend on the trip. Jesse for the first time had managed to receive £5 spending money from his father who had all week been in a jubilant mood. Fortunately for the pupils there were toilet facilities on site, as one of the pupils could be seen jiggling erratically, with an urgent need to make use of them. As the pupils made their way to the start of the trail, they were aligned in pairs.

Jesse was very fond of the natural surroundings and felt adventurously enchanted as they passed through denser areas of trees. Despite prior instruction to the pupils to proceed in an orderly fashion, two of the pupils began to hop like frogs over branches and fallen leaves. The two pupils had set a springing example, in which a number of the other pupils began to imitate the moves. Mrs Robbins quickly marched forward and put an immediate stop to it.

Although Toby was in a different group than Jesse, they found themselves crossing paths as the groups made their way through the trail. Upon noticing Jesse, Toby took his opportunity to throw insults and insisted that Jesse was a beetle on the floor that he could trample on.

As time moved on Jesse carried out his sprinkling on Toby as he walked by with his group. Toby's group was now fast approaching a diverting trail that included a muddy area that favoured a miniature swamp. Meanwhile, Glad was contentedly trekking through the trail on standby. Toby's group proceeded further up the trail. 'Be careful of the muddy area everyone!" Toby teacher informed them. 'Slip, slip, slip' to everyone's astonishment Toby had managed to completely slip over the muddy area. He was rendered drenched from head to toe in muddy waters. As he struggled to recompose himself, he now resembled a creature that Jesse once saw in a frightening movie involving a swamp. Jesse as well as his other classmates once again had the last laugh and now a clean-up project had to be fulfilled. Toby was just about in luck as one of the teachers had a spare set of dry clothes to hand for him to change into. Would Toby ever learn his personal lesson.

By lunch time the different groups had convened and they made their way to a reserved picnic area. Jesse and Daz sat together alongside a few of their friendly classmates. The joke of the day was still circulating around like wildfire and Toby was still feeling the emotional effects. As if the day couldn't get any better Elizabeth once again caught the eye of Jesse. This time she then stood up and walked over to him, whilst Jesse sat seemingly entranced. 'Oh my, did you see what happened earlier?" Elizabeth said.

"Er, yeah, when Toby was covered in mud, that was hilarious!" Jesse said excitedly. She then stretched out her hand to welcome a handshake.

"My name's Elizabeth by the way and your name is?"

"Er, er, my name is Jesse, I've seen you around the school sometimes!"

"Yeah, I've noticed you too, guess I've been meaning to say hello for a while!"

Elizabeth then took a seat beside him, whilst they continued their endearing conversation. Their friendly exchange of stories was set to blossom into a worthwhile friendship. Jesse went as far as to reward his newly found friend with a key-ring, with a portion of the £5 he had to spend at the gift shop. Likewise, she too bought him a small gift to honour the day.

A further day in the land of dreams saw the opening round of the sports day saga. Parents at the sidelines were anxious for the events to begin, where they could go on to capture their child's momentous moment. Team captains were being assigned and the team's were organised in line with their respective colours. Jesse's team were all in yellow, which was marvellous for him as that particular colour always reminded him of the sunshine his mother brought. Amongst the crowds was Jesse's father, who had turned up for the first time for a sports day event.

Jesse was beyond grateful for his arrival, yet was eager to compete, as sports was amongst his favourite activities. Jesse had been selected for the beanbag race and came second, in which the beanbags were kept 'level-headed' for the majority of participants. As further events unfolded Jesse triumphantly came first along with another pupil in the three-legged race. Winning cheers and joyful applause set the tone for the day.

The only seemingly downside was the continued venting of fury from Toby who didn't always seek sweet revenge. Whilst in the awaiting queues, he had voiced across his continued insults towards Jesse. Glad had already provided him with the necessary dust in the pocket of his shorts. As Jesse went over to fetch his water bottle he took the time to sprinkle the dust on Toby upon his return.

The entertaining egg and spoon race was about to get underway. Toby along with three competitors were in line at the start position. Each pupil had their egg all steady on their spoons, ready to begin. As the whistle blew, the race was off. On Toby's part there was only one continued drawback. With the dazzling dust unnoticed, his egg kept repeatedly dropping off his spoon. Every time in which he attempted to remount the egg was to no avail. He kept on trying , but with no such luck. The other pupils had each crossed the finishing line, leaving Toby still battling away at the start. In the end a nearby teacher had to bring that particular race to a close, in which the crowd gave him a round of applause for competing. By this time although Toby was boiling like a kettle on the inside, Jesse thought he would try to offer a resolution in the form of kindness.

The events were sailing through with sheer delight and the time had come for the ultimate final race - the relay. As Jesse was a competent runner he had been one of the first selected for the race. Three other pupils joined him at the start line, all of which included Toby who was positioned exactly in the next lane.

Jesse gathered up his thoughts in due concentration and looked ahead into the distance. A period of being situated right next to his rival felt like a lifetime. The whistle blew and seconds felt like whole minutes. Jesse edged on forward, as did Toby. This race was an extended form, which meant that they needed to run from the start line to the finishing line twice. The two of them were neck and neck on their way back to the start. Toby took a quick glance towards Jesse, but Toby then tripped and went flying with a sudden thump. Jesse upon this realisation experienced a mental pause. Should he continue and defeat is rival, or not? As micro-seconds flew by Jesse then stooped down, took Toby by the arm and helped him to his feet. He then continued to embrace his arm, in which they ran together with a mutual team spirit to cross the finishing line at the same time. The crowds that were seated stood in ovation as the entire audience cheered exuberantly.

Both Toby and Jesse gave each other a friendly hand shake and Toby said. "Actually, you're alright you are, you're really alight!" As the pupils went off to make way for the parent's race, Jesse was warmly welcomed by Elizabeth to his surprise. She instantly gave him a brief hug and congratulated him on his races, as well as for his noble act towards Toby.

As they stood on Jesse plucked up the courage to ask, "Elizabeth, would you be my girlfriend?"

"I absolutely will!" Elizabeth said.

It was a splendid day for all, in which Jesse was pleased to have established common ground with the focus of his admiration. He was later able to greet his father who was thrilled at his son's sporting experience. Meanwhile, Glad was dancing around ecstatically all around the field, to the amusement of Jesse.

The joy had returned and so Jesse had returned safe and sound from the land of dreams to his cosy bed. As he drew back the curtain, the morning sun came glistening in. He could hear the chirpy tweets of nearby birds, singing a new song. All was well in the world of Jesse and he now felt he could approach his school life with no dust required.

He followed through his established routine and got ready for his up and coming breakfast. He even started to pay more attention to grooming his hair, since he had a new best friend on the horizon.

"Jesse, breakfast is at the table." Suzie called. As he made his way downstairs, his parents were both seated in joyful readiness and his plate was all laid out. As this was not a school day, his mother gave him the option of different choices for breakfast. Jesse enjoyed steamed tomatoes topped with cheese, sausages, beans, poached egg and freshly squeezed juice. Suzie's flavoursome meals were well received , as was Jimmy's offer to wash up thereafter.

There was a clump at the door, the morning post had duly arrived. Aside from bills and further bills, was a brightly colourful envelope of a different kind. Jimmy rested the pile of post on the table and decided to open the colourful envelope first. As he opened the envelope to take a look at the contents, he took a pause and v-e-r-y s-l-o-w-l-y looked up towards Jesse.

"I can't believe it!" Jimmy said looking very stunned.

"Believe what?" Suzie asked.

"The prize draw that we enter every month, you know the one for the charities. We've won dear, a car dear, we've won!" As they read through the accompanying details, they had in fact been selected for the prize.

"As I said son, once this car is sold, that money is for you as well as your education." Jimmy noted. That was his promise that day, which was soon fulfilled in the weeks that followed.

The new car was put up for sale, was sold at speed and the cash proceeds were duly invested in Jesse. As well as educational funds, Jesse was soon rewarded with a very desired football kit, new clothes for his wardrobe and a sturdy new bike.

The whole family took exciting trips back to the valley and beyond, in which they participated in a variety of activities. Jesse was enjoying quality family time, recreational time, as well as having an enhanced school experience.

With the help and enthusiasm of Glad he was able to open up a whole new world of possibilities and adventure. As Jesse had become more confident and self assured in the land of dreams, he had in turn become more at peace in real-time. He had a sharper focus and was able to embrace the here and now, with an amazing insight, especially with the people he was fond of the most!

Written by

Geraldine

Taylor

15658978R00053

Printed in Great Britain
by Amazon